DIANA: ALONE AGAINST THE SEA

DIANA: ALONE AGAINST THE SEA

Valjean McLenighan

Illustrated by Jay Blair

RAINTREE PUBLISHERS
Milwaukee • Toronto • Melbourne • London

Library of Congress Number: 79-21518

1 2 3 4 5 6 7 8 9 0 84 83 82 81 80

Printed and bound in the United States of America.

Library of Congress Cataloging in Publication Data

McLenighan, Valjean.
    Diana: alone against the sea.

    SUMMARY: A biographical account of the American marathon swimmer with emphasis on the 41 hours she spent in the ocean in an attempt to swim from Cuba to Florida.
    1.   Nyad, Diana — Juvenile literature.   2.   Swimmers — United States — Biography — Juvenile literature.
[1.   Nyad, Diana.   2.   Swimmers]   I.   Blair, Jay.
II.   Title.
GV838.N9M32   797.2'1'0294   [B]   [92]   79-21518
ISBN 0-8172-1557-3 lib. bdg.

The publisher thanks Random House, Inc. and Ms. Magazine Corporation for permission to reprint the following:

Pages 9, 10, 27, and 41. Excerpts from *Other Shores* by Diana Nyad. © 1978 by Diana Nyad. Published by Random House, Inc.

Page 47. Excerpt from "Diana Nyad: the Obsession of the Long-Distance Swimmer" by Jane Shapiro, which appeared in *Ms.*, August, 1978. © 1978 by Ms. Magazine Corporation.

CONTENTS

CHAPTER 1

The Nearly Impossible Goal

Diana Nyad sat back on her heels. "This is it," she said to herself. "This is the swim that will make history!" For three weeks Diana's living room floor had been covered with maps. They showed every major body of water in the world. The champion swimmer was searching for a route. Diana wanted to make a swim that would break every long-distance record in the book. She wanted to do something so nearly impossible that it could not be matched for many years.

For days on end, Diana bent over the maps and charts in her New York apartment. She made list after list of distances, water temperatures, wind speeds, and currents. Each day she crossed out certain places and added new ones. Finally, in April 1977, her goal came into view.

She would swim nonstop from Cuba to Florida — 130 miles through shark-filled waters. The crossing would take her sixty hours, maybe sixty-five. That's a day, a night, a second day and night, plus another twelve to seventeen hours!

Think how hard it would be just to stay awake that long. Then imagine trying to *swim* for sixty hours without resting and with no help. No flippers, floats, or wet suits are permitted in an official marathon (long-distance) swim. The swimmer may not touch the boat or any other person at any time. There is no protection from wind or waves. The swimmer has nothing to rely on but her or his own strength.

Cuba to Florida! The idea fired Diana's imagination. The going record for an open-water swim was 60 miles across Lake Michigan in 34 hours, 38 minutes. There were other milestones in swim-

ming history. But nothing compared with the adventure Diana had in mind.

It was a bold idea. But then so is Diana. "My world view is dramatic," she writes. "Every minute seems like the most important minute of my life."

She has always felt that way. When she was ten, Diana Nyad wrote an essay called, "What I Will Do for the Rest of My Life." One of her goals was to become a great athlete. "I need to practice every day," she wrote. "I need to sleep as little as possible. I need to read at least one major book a week. And I need to remember that my . . . years are going to go by too quickly."

Diana won two state swimming championships by the time she was twelve. Her sights were set on the 1968 Olympics. But a heart ailment struck the summer after her junior year in high school, 1966. Diana needed months of bed rest. It was a full year before she recovered. At the age of sixteen, her Olympic hopes were smashed.

While her body healed, Diana exercised her mind. She read story after story about people who survived the most extreme hardships. One of her favorites was about a man who was buried alive under four feet of snow for a week and survived twenty-seven days without food.

That story and others made a lasting impression on Diana. In college she became a professional marathon swimmer. "What interests me about marathon swimming is that it tests the human spirit," Diana said. "It is a sport of extremes."

Marathon swimming is one of the most difficult sports in the world. Athletes train hard for months to get ready for the tortures of mind and body that are part of any long race. Each year between January and October, the best marathon swimmers in the world compete in a series of contests. Businesses and sometimes governments of countries put up the prize money. In some cases the sponsors also cover a swimmer's air fare and other expenses. The first race each season is held in Australia. The swimmers also compete in Europe, North and South America, and the Caribbean.

On the professional racing circuit between 1970 and 1975, Diana set a world record for crossing Lake Ontario. She also set women's records for the Bay of Naples, Argentina's Paraná River, and the fifty miles from Australia's Great Barrier Reef to the coast. In 1974 she was the official women's world champion.

Long-distance swimming isn't an exciting sport to watch, as are football or tennis. It's one painful stroke after another, hour after agonizing hour. The only really thrilling moment is when the swimmer finally reaches the other shore. In some countries, such as Egypt, tens of thousands of fans gather at the finish line to watch the swimmers struggle ashore.

And the prize money isn't great. Other countries pay their swimmers to join the professional tour in hopes of capturing a championship. But it doesn't work that way in America. After six years on the pro tour, Diana was a world champion. But her prize money barely covered her air fare to and from races. Except for her fellow swimmers and a few loyal sports writers and fans, no one had ever heard of Diana Nyad. Diana began to realize that promoters and sponsors of races were the ones who made the money and got all the attention. Swimmers worked their hearts out just to meet their expenses.

In 1975 Diana quit the pro tour in disgust. She was twenty-five years old and tired of working so hard and being so poor. It was time to make herself known in the world and to earn a little money. Diana hired a business manager. On October 6, 1975, she swam around Manhattan Island in 7 hours and 57 minutes. It was a fairly easy swim for Diana. But it set a new record, and more important, made her an instant celebrity. Rich and famous people suddenly wanted to meet her.

Diana's next project was a double crossing of the English Channel, scheduled for late summer, 1976. Just for trying the swim, she earned more

money than she had in six years on the marathon tour. But Diana failed to beat the Channel, though she tried three different times that summer.

She began to wonder if the thrill of marathon swimming was gone. She had spent years becoming a champion of one of the most demanding sports on earth. Perhaps the time had come to focus on a new goal.

But before she retired, Diana wanted to set one last record. She would make a swim so glorious and so difficult that it would outshine every other marathon in history.

Diana spent weeks in a feverish search for a route. Finally she settled on the most extraordinary goal any swimmer had ever chosen. She would make the swim from Cuba to Florida.

A Year to Go

Diana figured she had about a 50–50 chance of making it. With luck, and if the wind and weather were on her side, she felt the odds might be 75–25. Others were not so sure.

There are several problems with a Cuba-to-Florida swim besides its length. The biggest problem is the Gulf Stream — a powerful current, twenty-five miles wide, that flows from west to east between Cuba and the Florida Keys. The stream follows no regular pattern from day to day. On some days it is just off the Cuban coast. On other days it flows much farther north, parallel to the Florida Keys. The average speed of the current is three knots — that's a little over three miles per hour — and it is faster than the average long-distance swimming speed. At its swiftest point the Gulf Stream tops five knots.

There's no way to swim between Florida and Cuba without going through the Gulf Stream.

Diana knew that how and where she crossed it could mean the difference between success and failure. The ideal would be to start the swim when the stream was flowing close to the Cuban shore. That way she would be at her strongest for the battle. If she caught the current in the middle of the swim, with the wind against her, she might have to head directly west, instead of north, in order to keep from being pulled off course. That would cost her time and precious strength.

The Gulf Stream also causes rough water. It's a lot more work to swim through waves than through smooth water. Hours of bobbing and tossing almost always lead to seasickness. A

swimmer can't help swallowing a certain amount of water during a marathon try. Gulp after gulp of saltwater means certain agony. Diana would have to get the best weather and navigation advice she could find. High winds whipping up the choppy waters of the Gulf Stream would mean big trouble, and maybe even disaster.

Jellyfish would be another problem. Although there are many jellyfish in the warm waters between Cuba and Florida, they are hard to see — especially at night. Diana isn't allergic to their stings, as some swimmers are. But she feels pain the same as anyone else. A stinging encounter with a jellyfish takes quite some time to stop hurting.

Diana would also be subject to surprise attacks by sea gulls. They are likely to swoop down and peck at a swimming cap, mistaking it for a fish. The birds are easily chased off with a swipe of the hand. But a sudden swoosh of wings around the face and sharp peck on the head can turn the trance-like fatigue of a long swim into a living nightmare.

Diana had dealt with jellyfish and sea gulls on other swims. They could hurt and frighten, but they weren't deadly. Diana knew that her most serious problem would be sharks.

In some waters, such as those off the coast of Mexico, a person with a rifle aboard the crew boat

is enough to take care of any threat. But the waters between Cuba and Florida have many sharks. Also, Diana would be swimming through two full nights. And crew members with rifles wouldn't be much help after dark. Shark repellents are supposed to keep sharks away from people. But they have not been proved safe. So there was no way around it: she would have to use a shark cage.

Diana hated the idea. A few years before, she had been forced to use a shark cage for a swim off Australia's Great Barrier Reef. The cage was a bulky, wire mesh affair, shaped like a room that was too small. Diana had to stop every few strokes to keep herself in the middle. Fumes from the boat pulling the cage made her sick. After hours of struggling to stay clear of the walls, she accidentally smashed into the front of the cage. Diana has a powerful stroke, and the accident broke three of her fingers. She finally reached the coast, but at great cost. The shark cage, she figured, had added an extra six hours — and a great deal of pain — to the swim.

Still, she couldn't have made it at all without the cage. Sharks brushed the sides and bottom throughout the twenty-four hours of the Australian swim. Diana knew she needed the protection. So she would have to have a cage designed and built especially for this swim.

Diana took her ideas for a shark cage to Rich du Moulin. He was a friend and sailor who had made a name for himself in the international racing world. Diana wanted the cage to have its own engines. She knew it would be impossible to swim for sixty hours behind a boat belching gas fumes. The cage also had to be large enough so that she wouldn't be crashing into the walls all the time. It had to have space for a driver and trainers.

With du Moulin and Ken Gunderson, an experienced sailor, Diana came up with a design for a cage. It was forty feet long, twenty feet wide, and twelve feet deep. The cage would be made of steel tubing and plastic-coated, chain-linked fencing. It would hang from two pontoons, each three feet wide. And it would have two pairs of 75-horse-power engines. The pontoons and front and back walls would be rubberized. A bridge above the back of the rig would be big enough for a driver, several others, plus communications equipment.

Diana's swim around Manhattan Island had been made with nothing more than a borrowed boat. But the Cuba swim was something else entirely. The shark cage alone would cost at least $42,000 to build. Other expenses would bring the cost of the swim to more than $100,000. Diana needed trainers, navigators, and someone to manage everything. Some of her friends offered to work for free. Still, their food, housing, and transportation would cost money.

For the next year, Diana's mind was filled with almost nothing but the swim. When she wasn't training, she was busy working out the countless details of the project. Where would she get the money? She would have to find a good business manager. Then she'd have to organize a team. She needed expert navigation. It was important to get the right trainers. Then there was the shark cage — someone would have to make sure that it was built properly and on time. Arrangements would have to be made with the Cuban government. And someone would have to handle the press.

Training in Danger

Diana began training on July 1, 1977 — a year before she planned to make the swim. For the first six months she ran from ten to twelve miles every day. By January she could run twelve miles in seventy-two minutes — six minutes a mile. She skipped rope for an hour a day, and twice a week she worked out on special training equipment. On top of all this, she played two to four hours of squash every day, just because she wanted to get good at the game. By the end of the season, in February 1978, she was the top-ranked woman player in New York. She had also just about finished her first book, *Other Shores*, the story of her life.

February saw some other developments as well. Diana hired a new business manager — her fourth since the Manhattan swim. George Wallach was said to be one of the best sports agents in the business. He had a big job cut out for him.

Wallach had to find a company to put up the money for the shark cage right away. And by July 1, he had to raise more than $100,000.

With Wallach on board, and the squash season behind her, Diana began what she called "serious training" on February 27. She left the land for the water — five hours of swimming a day, then six, then eight. Except for six weeks at an Olympic pool in California, Diana trained in public pools around Manhattan, including the West Side Y. There she had to keep a constant lookout for amateurs who didn't know what they were doing. The year before, one of them had broken her jaw with a frog kick.

Despite these problems, Diana was in top physical shape by May 1. She was ready to begin the last and most intense phase of her training. Diana's schedule called for two months of ocean swimming to get ready for Cuba. Working out in a pool, even for eight-hour stretches, is a lot easier than churning through open water.

Early in June they would start testing the shark cage. One of the runs would be a twenty-four-hour swim with a full crew. Early in July, Diana would be ready for Cuba. All she would have to do then would be to rest up in Havana and wait for good weather.

That was the plan. But what happened was something else. By May 1, Diana was frantic. She didn't even have air fare to get to Florida, much less money for a shark cage. Business agent Wallach had arranged meeting after meeting with oil companies, soap companies, you name it. They liked Diana. But the world of high finance moves slowly.

Diana waited in agony for someone to decide to sponsor the swim. If she wasn't in saltwater by the third week of May, she knew she may as well forget Cuba. Day after day passed with no decision. By the middle of May Diana was so discouraged that she couldn't even drag herself to a pool. But one afternoon the Colgate Company came through with $42,000. It was just enough to get the shark cage and the ocean training under way.

At least one big worry was off her mind. Diana headed for Florida with two of her trainers. Margie Carroll, the head trainer, was Diana's former student. The two had met in 1975, when Diana coached the swimming team at Barnard College. Jean Goldin, a nurse, was an old friend who had been along on many other swims. Candace Lyle Hogan, Diana's New York roommate joined the crew later that summer.

The women set up headquarters in Miami Beach. They settled into a routine of daily long, hard swims in open water.

"Those training swims were much more dangerous than the Cuba swim," Candace re-

calls. Diana swam without a cage. The waters off the Florida coast were full of sharks, and Diana was warned never to swim beyond a depth of fifteen feet. Her trainers, alongside in a rubber boat, had to keep a constant watch for sharks. They were forever nosing Diana closer to the shore.

Candace well remembers one long swim through the canal leading into Lake Okeechobee. Margie Carroll was driving the boat, and Candace was keeping a lookout for alligators. "They're not dangerous on the banks," she explains. "Only when they're crossing from one side to the other." Suddenly Candace looked up to see a "log with eyes" crossing about twelve feet in front of Diana. She blew a shrill blast on her whistle and prayed that Diana would hear her. Fortunately, Diana did, and she quickly scrambled into the boat.

Diana's trainers kept an eye out for her safety in the water. They saw that she ate well and got enough rest, and they shared in planning the swim. But most important, they were fellow travelers on Diana's remarkable journey of the mind. They knew the tricks that long hours in the water can play on a swimmer's brain.

After ten hours or so, Diana loses most of her senses. Half blinded by goggles, she can barely see. Layers of swim caps block out most sound.

Taste and smell are destroyed by the saltwater.
Long hours of cold numb the sense of touch.
Under this stress, the mind begins to wander.
Diana starts to lose concentration and become

depressed. Finally she enters a trance-like state. She describes it in her book, *Other Shores*.

"As far as you know, you are in the middle of nowhere and any effort you might produce to stroke again won't necessarily bring you any closer to your goal because much of the time you can't seem to remember what the goal is. It is clear that your ordeal is without end, and there is only one thing you somehow sense — that the choice to abandon the struggle and climb aboard

the ship would be to fragment your pride beyond repair. Survival is keeping one's dignity intact."

For her trainers Diana chose people who understood the nature of her struggle and were experienced in the special madness of a marathon swim. Once, during a long swim in Argentina, Diana imagined she was being attacked and eaten alive by sea gulls. Her trainer didn't try to talk Diana out of her nightmare — or out of the water. Instead she joined in the fantasy and came to Diana's rescue, pretending to beat the birds off with an oar.

This was the kind of understanding Diana looked for in her trainers. They were as much spiritual coaches as anything else. Diana had complete faith in Margie Carroll and the other five trainers who would work the Cuba swim. By the end of June, she knew she was ready in body, mind, and spirit.

Unfortunately, the business end of the swim was in much worse shape.

CHAPTER 4

Sixty Hours to Florida

Money problems hounded the Cuba swim from beginning to end. They delayed the start of ocean training. Lack of funds put the shark cage behind schedule. As the July target date loomed closer, expenses mounted higher than anyone had planned. The final cost of the swim came to $176,000.

The lack of money lent an air of constant crisis to the swim. As late as the second week in July, when Diana should have been resting and gaining weight in Cuba, she was running around New York in a last-ditch search for funds. Colgate raised its support to $77,000. Several other companies — including Dannon, Perrier, Murdock News, and Germany's *Stern* magazine — put up lesser amounts. But Diana resented the energy she had to devote to raising money. She felt that George Wallach had let her down. She wasn't happy with the firm he had hired to handle press

relations. And the swim ended up putting her $15,000 in debt.

"Sports agents are lazy characters," Diana fumed. "They don't really want to work for you. All they want to do is answer phones."

Diana was happier with her choice of an operations manager. George Post was a yacht broker who had been recommended by Rich du Moulin for the job of overseeing the swim. Diana felt he did a fine job handling the hundreds of details. Post kept calm in the face of the tempest over the money. He made sure the shark cage was built well and quickly. He persuaded the Mercury company to donate the motors to power it. He also made arrangements for Diana's free hotel suite and was able to get many other things free.

It was during the summer test runs that an argument arose over Diana's use of the shark cage. The World Professional Marathon Swimming Federation objected to the cage and refused to approve the swim. Diana was furious. She said that she would make the swim anyway. But she did remove a "snowplow" device on the front of the cage that could be lowered to sweep away jellyfish. She felt it might give her an advantage by breaking up the waves. "I've never cheated in my entire career, and I did not want anything that would help me in any way," she said.

The uproar over the shark cage was upsetting enough. But the tension rose even higher when the Cuban government did not respond to Diana's request for permission to start the swim from its shores. The swim had already been put back to July 21. More delays could kill it altogether. Every day that Diana waited for permission brought her closer to hurricane season.

July passed without word from Cuba. Officials were busy with a giant youth festival and with getting ready for Cuba's independence celebration, July 26. No one had time to deal with permissions and visas for a crew of thirty Americans trailed by a press corps of almost the same size.

As the delays dragged on, the press began to get restless. The sports writers and TV people were used to covering well-organized events that started on time. But July rolled into August with no swim. Deadlines were set, cancelled, and set again. Travel plans were made and unmade.

Equipment was misplaced or broken. Communications broke down.

Finally, permission to enter Cuba arrived. There was a mad scramble for Ortegaso Beach, which was fifty miles west of Havana. But by that time the swim had begun to fall apart. Ken Gunderson, a key navigator, was still in Florida when Diana stepped into the water. With him was the woman who was supposed to handle the news people.

"It was one crisis after another," trainer Candace Hogan recalls. "Just before we were ready to take off, somebody realized that we hadn't even thought about life jackets."

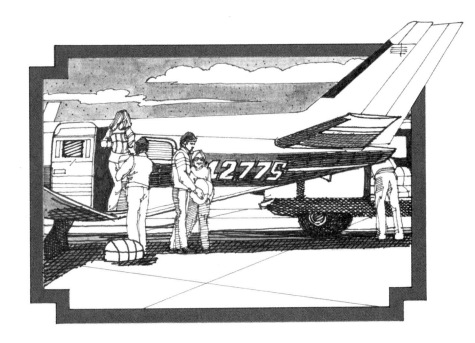

By August 13, Diana couldn't wait any longer. The water was rippling with three-foot waves. It was not the calm Diana had hoped for. But the longer she waited, the greater the risk was that strong winds would drive the waves even higher.

Reporters and photographers surrounded her as she walked into the water. Yet Diana looked very lonely. At its heart, a marathon swim is one person's struggle against an all-powerful opponent. Diana knew that no one really conquers "Her Majesty, the Sea." The best she could hope for was not to be defeated.

At 2:07 P.M. on Sunday, she left Ortegaso Beach. "I feel ready," she said. "Goodbye. I guess I'll see you all in about two and a half days."

CHAPTER 5

The Middle of Nowhere

"This is the worst night of my life," Diana groaned. "My God, if it's this bad after only twelve hours . . ."

The weather was against her from the start. The wind was supposed to have died at sundown. But it gusted at a steady fifteen knots (more than seventeen miles per hour) into Sunday night and well into Monday morning. Three-foot waves washed through the shark cage and then smacked back again. Diana was tossed from side to side.

Seasickness was a terrible problem for the first twelve hours. Diana couldn't manage to keep any food down at all. She grew weak from battling nausea as well as the waves. And she lost the benefit of her hourly feedings by vomiting them up.

Jellyfish stung her throughout the night. Diana screamed when they brushed against her. Her trainers tried to help by bathing the stings in ammonia.

"It takes a lot of concentration and attention to

35

be a trainer," Candace Hogan says. "It's amazing that Diana can see you at all, through foggy goggles, at night, with her eyes swollen. But you can communicate through the eyes, and it means a good deal to her."

Trainers aboard the shark cage, called the *Cleopatra*, were supposed to work in groups of three. One would ride on the driver's platform and fix Diana's high-energy snacks, and feed them to her. Two others were supposed to sit on the pontoons next to Diana, watching her and keeping her on course with hand signals. Shifts

were supposed to change every two to four hours.

But the wind was so bad that the trainers worked through meals and rest periods. All six were on board the *Cleopatra*, giving Diana support.

At 4:00 A.M. her trainers played tapes of Simon and Garfunkel songs. The music blasted into the night. During one song, Diana said to Margie Carroll, "That means there are no more heroes, right?"

Margie told her that if she made the swim, *she* would be one.

Candace Hogan recalls Diana's remarkable victory over seasickness. "I sat there on the pontoon and watched her make up her mind to beat it. And after about fifteen hours she got over being seasick. She was feeling good about herself. Her mind was set. She made a decision to win."

At dawn on Monday, August 14, Diana managed to keep some food down — chicken and soda water with dextrose. Her strength returned as the sun rose. She asked manager George Post to see that everyone in the press corps got a chance to visit the shark cage.

More than half a dozen boats carrying crew and press were following Diana. But there was only room on the *Cleopatra* for a few reporters at a time. Those on the press boats had to get to the cage by means of a small boat. The rivalry among the press was intense. Everyone was competing for a story. At one point Diana saw a reporter on the shark cage actually shove and kick another reporter who was trying to board the *Cleopatra*.

There was no one on the swim taking care of the press. The woman who was supposed to be doing the job was still in Florida! She and navigator Ken Gunderson were to come out to the shark cage in a motor boat. But they couldn't find Diana in the high seas. And it didn't help matters when the *Cleopatra*'s radio went out.

The members of the press had to fend for themselves. For them the swim was a disaster. Many were as seasick as Diana. By Monday morning the waves were up to four feet. They continued to swell as the day went on.

The crew from one TV network had all its equipment aboard the *Proud Mary*, a chartered boat. When they plugged it in, they blew out the boat's electrical system. The boat started to leak, but the pump wouldn't work. Finally the Coast Guard was called to the rescue.

By Monday night, the waves were higher than six feet. The Coast Guard ordered all boats out of the water. But the *Cleopatra* ignored the order. Waves slapped Diana around as though she were a piece of driftwood. Jellyfish struck her in the mouth. Her lips and tongue swelled to twice normal size.

"Tonight won't be as bad as last night, will it?" Diana asked Candace. "I couldn't stand anything like last night."

From the platform, Candace gently crumbled chicken meat into Diana's mouth. Suddenly Diana's hands shot into the air.

"I thought I saw a barracuda in the bottom of the cage," she said.

"There are no barracudas here," Candace answered.

As the night wore on, Diana's trainers became seriously worried about her swollen mouth. By the time they decided to send for a doctor, the *Cleopatra*'s radio was gone. A small boat carried the message over to one of the press boats. The

tiny craft had to fight its way back through the high seas with the Coast Guard's reply.

Officials thought the group was crazy to be out in such weather. There was no way they could get a doctor to the shark cage in waves that sometimes topped eight feet. "The proper treatment is for the swimmer to get out of the water," the Coast Guard replied.

But Diana pushed on. "You want to quit so many times," she wrote. "But there is a quiet burning near the heart that makes you clench your teeth and refuse to go out a quitter. You roll over on your back, you throw off your goggles, you say no, you sigh, you cry, and the quiet burning somehow makes you roll back over and pick the left arm up again."

CHAPTER 6

I've Tried So Hard

Diana was supposed to swim north to the Gulf Stream, then cut to the northwest and come out of the water at Key West. But the shark cage caught the wind like a sail. It was hard to tell exactly where they were. By late Monday the crew knew the *Cleopatra* was far off course. During one six-hour stretch, Diana actually fell back a couple of miles.

She was still swimming strongly when Tuesday dawned. But after forty hours in the water, she was seeing things. She thought the shark cage had turned into a cave from which there was no escape. Her hands, bleached white by the ocean, looked like claws. Diana's tongue hung lifelessly from her mouth.

They were still some eighty miles from Key West. Diana had already covered close to that distance. But the *Cleopatra* had been blown in a circle that left it only fifty miles from the start.

Diana's trainers knew it was hopeless. Around seven o'clock Tuesday morning, they sent for the reporters.

Margie Carroll broke the news to Diana. "Everything's gone wrong, Diana. You can't make it. It's not your fault."

"But couldn't I keep going?" Diana whispered painfully. "If I swam for forty more hours, couldn't I make it then?"

"The wind is too strong against you," said Rich du Moulin. "The waves are too high, and three of the four engines on the shark cage are flooded. No swimmer could make it now, not even you."

"But I can't quit now," Diana cried. "You don't understand. Isn't there another place to swim for, some island, maybe?"

"No, Diana. Key West is still the closest point."

Diana burst into tears. "I'm sorry," she wept. "I tried so hard. I've never done anything so hard in my whole life."

Diana's friends pulled her from the water forty-one hours and forty-seven minutes after she had entered it. Soon she was speeding to Key West, sound asleep in the escort boat.

Perhaps things would have been different if Ken Gunderson had not been stranded in Florida. He was an experienced sailor. Candace Hogan describes him as an "earthy, Humphrey Bogart type who knew how to navigate by the seat of his pants." Du Moulin, on the other hand, "never got his hair wet." He was used to sailing with fancy equipment and charts, not to battling the high seas in pre-hurricane season.

Du Moulin explained that the Gulf Stream is complex and that the wind was a constant problem.

"Rich did the best he could," Diana said. "But the navigation could have been better."

Candace said later that the weather was too hard for the navigators. "But maybe it would have been impossible for anyone," she added.

Nearly everyone agrees that Diana could have made the swim if the weather had been with her.

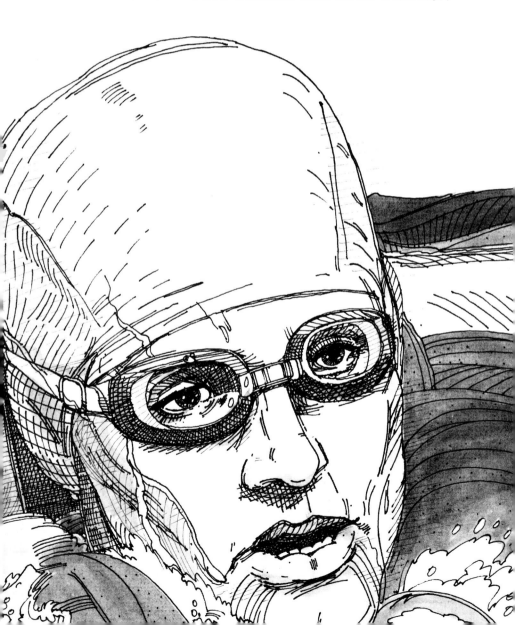

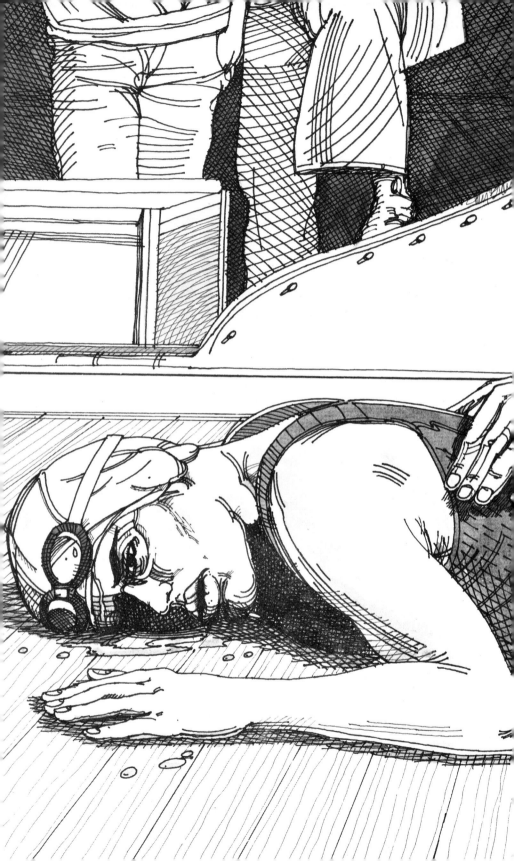

In fact, Diana intends to try the swim again. "I dream of seeing the Florida coast," Diana told a reporter. "And I dream of hearing people, hearing voices — the way you do way off in the fog — that are yelling and saying Bravo! and all that.

"And there I am: seeing the white sand, and going so slowly that it seems as though it will take me another sixty hours. But it doesn't matter any more. It matters so much in the middle. As long as you can see the end, you know you're going to get there. No matter how slowly you go."